THERE WAS A MONKEY

CAROLYN RUBERTO

Balboa Press books may be ordered through booksellers or by contacting:

Balboa Press
A Division of Hay House
1663 Liberty Drive
Bloomington, IN 47403
www.balboapress.com.au
1 (877) 407-4847

Because of the dynamic nature of the Internet, any web addresses or links contained in this book may have changed since publication and may no longer be valid. The views expressed in this work are solely those of the author and do not necessarily reflect the views of the publisher, and the publisher hereby disclaims any responsibility for them.

Any people depicted in stock imagery provided by Getty Images are models, and such images are being used for illustrative purposes only.
Certain stock imagery © Getty Images.

ISBN: 978-1-5043-1618-7 (sc)
ISBN: 978-1-5043-1617-0 (e)

Print information available on the last page.

Balboa Press rev. date: 03/11/2019

BALBOA
PRESS
A DIVISION OF HAY HOUSE

Dedicated to my Son, Anthony

There was a monkey

And there was a tree.

The tallest tree you would ever see.

And the monkey said to himself with glee,

"If I climb up high to the top of that tree

I'll see the whole world below me," thought he,

"And I'll be the bravest a monkey can be".

So he climbed and he climbed

Stopping halfway for tea

Thinking out loud to himself,

"This can never be!

I'm far too tired to climb to the top

I must admit I'll have to stop."

So he stopped for a rest
And slept through the night
And when the sun rose
He got quite a fright.
For next to him there, on the branch of the tree,
Was a horse sitting there smiling quite happily.

"Good morning to you," said the horse politely.
"I'm happy to meet you," replied the monkey.
"My idea was the same as yours," said the horse
"But I climbed this far and got stuck. Of course,
I'm not good at climbing but I thought I'd try still.
You can do so much if you have a strong will."
The monkey agreed and they continued to speak
 Until together they decided to climb to the peak.

A few branches higher they stopped for a chat
When who should come up but a big tabby cat.
"How do you do?" said the cat with a gleam.
"You wouldn't, by chance, have a saucer of cream?"
"I'm afraid we do not," replied the monkey,
"But you're welcome to have a cup of our tea."
"We're on our way to the top of this tree.
We'll be the bravest horse and monkey.
We'll see the whole world from the very top
But how come we find you in such a spot?"

"Dear, oh dear. Why, haven't you heard?
The reason I'm here is I'm after a bird.
A bird with red feathers sounds delicious to me
And rumor has it he has a nest in this tree".
"That's not very nice," said the horse with disgust.
"Why don't you forget it and come on with us?
Together we'll climb to the top, just we three,
And we'll be the bravest that we all can be."

The cat agreed with a sly nod and wink

But knowing the cat, what's one to think?

It's in their nature to go after a bird.

No matter what anyone's told you or heard.

So they all climbed willingly, anxious to see

This big, wide world from the top of that tree.

As the afternoon came and the sun blazed down,

They drank some tea and handed cheesecake around.

"This is an adventure," the monkey started to say.

"I've had such a lovely, lovely day."

The horse replied for he was the wisest of all,

"That's all very well. I just hope we don't fall."

The monkey and cat felt there'd be no danger of that.

But the horse, well you see, was a timid old chap.

"Let's get on with it now," said the cat with a grin.

"You see I have to catch er.. finish what I begin."

So, on they went until evening came round

When all of them noticed there wasn't a sound.

Not a bump or a whistle or a tweet or a beep.

Why, it seemed the whole world had gone off to sleep.

"It's because we've climbed up so very high."

The monkey said," I can touch the sky."

The horse remarked it was still too far.

Just take a look at that twinkling star.

How pretty it looks but it's further away

Than we'll ever climb in just one day."

They continued their climb the very next morn,

Not one of them minding that it was just dawn.

So anxious were they to get on their way

They wouldn't waste one precious second of day.

Suddenly nothing was clear and the horse cried out loud.

"Good gracious my friends. We've climbed into a cloud!

We'd best stop right here as we can't see to go.

There's a danger we might fall right off here you know."

"Don't worry about that," said a strange voice from the fog.

And, to their amazement, out stepped a large dog.

"My sense of direction is perfect, you know.

I'd be happy to show you which way you can go."

All were most pleased to meet this new friend
Except for the cat whose fur stood on end.
The one thing he hated was dogs of all types
And this one especially looked like he might bite.
"Don't worry cat. I won't chase after you.
I have other more important things I must do.
I've come to check the view from this height.
I have a house to guard. See that place on the right?"

And lo and behold through a space in the fog
They could indeed see the house of this dog.
"But it's so far away," the monkey had to remark.
"No-one would hear the loudest of barks."
"Yes, I've gone a bit far," said the dog with a whine.
"But I couldn't resist climbing higher each time.
I'm quite proud of the way I've climbed up this tree
And when I heard voices I just had to see
If others had climbed for the same reason as me."

They proceeded to tell their tales each one by one

Until soon the fog parted and out came the sun.

The cat seemed quite anxious and started to say,

"Now we can see, please let's not delay.

I think I see feathers er.. flowers up here.

Make this one jump. You have nothing to fear."

And with agility true to cats of all types,

He made a great leap with no fear of height.

The monkey as well made this jump with great ease.

They're agile and fit and used to such trees.

But for the dog and the horse it was alas just too far.

"We'll never reach that. Let's just stay where we are."

"I won't hear of it," said the monkey, their friend.

"You can't come this far and not make the end.

We're nearly there. I can just see the top.

Reach out for my arm. I won't let you drop."

The cat was amused by all this, for you see,

To him, climbing was as easy as one, two and three.

He laughed at their tries and with a quick backward glance

Scampered further above them and started to dance.

He sang out loud as the dog clambered up

And laughed 'til he burst when the horse became stuck.

"You be careful, silly cat," said the horse angrily.

You're not that clever. You can fall from this tree."

But the cat just laughed louder until tears came to his eyes

And to show what he thought he just reached for the sky.

He stood on tip toe and wriggled a bit

And then with a great yelp did a double back flip!

But, what came without warning, was wind that day

Which shook the large branch and caused it to sway.

So that after his dance, to the amusement of all,

The cat lost his balance and started to fall.

One by one through the branches he crashed in great fright.

After a meow and a help he was soon out of sight.

Then, out of the blue, like a flash of bright light,

Came a beautiful bird, its red wings in full flight.

The rest of its body was yellow and green.

A more remarkable bird you would never have seen.

With a swoop so graceful it had them in awe,

It flew down to the cat and grasped at his paw.

The cat hung on mightily as he must know

That at this great height it's not wise to let go!

With the cat in its claws, the bird flew up and then down.

The cat gave a meow but it wouldn't slow down.

With a sharp turn and a dive the bird still flew around.

It didn't appear that it would ever touch ground.

"Oh dear," thought the cat, with fear in his eyes,
"Is this the bird I hoped to surprise?"
"How could I have thought to make it my tea?
More likely than not this bird will eat me!"
The bird then spoke quite politely at that,
"I know why you came here, Mr Cat.
I'm tired of being chased and hunted for fun.
I just want to live here and play in the sun."
"Oh do let me down," said the cat with a plea.
"I've learnt my lesson. Please set me free!"

The bird gracefully alighted right next to the horse
And set the cat down who was full of remorse.
The horse said, "I told you but you wouldn't listen to me."
And the cat was ashamed as all show offs should be.
"Well," said the monkey, "let's not argue at that.
We have a new friend and all's well with the cat."
The bird introduced himself to each one
And explained to them all he was there to have fun.
"Well so are we all. Just we three
Started this venture to climb this tree
And now we're here I'm anxious to see
This magnificent view from this very tall tree.

So they climbed and they climbed then stopped in awe
 For they realised then they could climb no more.
All around them, down below,
The earth in its glory was all aglow.
The setting sun was shedding its rays
Pink, orange and yellow and the distant haze
Was coloured with this radiant light.
It was a magical world this time before night.
Then slowly, so slowly, out peeped a small star.
First one then another gave its light from afar.
Like diamonds they sparkled and lit up the night
And the huge moon bathed them in silvery light.
They were sure they could touch it but none wanted to try,
All were transfixed by this beautiful sky.

They looked down then yet speak they could not
So magical was the sight from this spot.
A fairyland was spread far below
And twinkling lights with a welcoming glow
From firesides in houses small and neat.
The street lamps lighting each winding street.
Each was so moved by this wondrous sight
None wanted to break the silence that night

So they sat and they sat and watched the sun rise

And the world awakened before their eyes.

And as the sun shone on the world down below,

They realised then they would soon have to go.

The cat yawned and stretched then licked his fur.

"We should make our way down now," he said with a purr.

The monkey and dog agreed silently

But each secretly wishing to stay in that tree.

"My family will miss me, you know. Of course

I'd like to stay but I can't," said the horse.

The bird who was happily fluttering nearby

Flew up to them then and said with a cry,

"I have an idea! Now we are good friends

It would be sad to leave and not meet again.

So, what do you think at this time each year

If we climb this tree and meet right up here?"

So joyful were they at this very fine thought

They started to dance, with the bird for support.

Until tiredness crept over each one

And down they climbed slowly in the warmth of the sun.

As the time came for each one to depart,

They said goodbye but with joy in their hearts.

Each said to the next, "Now, don't be late!

Same time next year. I just can't wait!"

So, if you're out walking and see a tall tree
It could be the one where our friends like to be.
Of course they're only there once a year
But let me know if you see them for I hear
They're going to find something else to do
And I'd like to go with them.

Well, wouldn't you?

To Think About...

- **Which character is your favorite? Why?**

- **Why were each of them in the tree?**

- **What are the two reasons the monkey wanted to climb the tree?**

- **Have you ever been brave like these characters?**

- **Is there something you want to do that will require you to be brave?**

- Many stories have villains.
  Why might you think the cat is a villain?

- This story is about friends helping each other.
  Do your friends help you and do you help them?

- **Why is the cat not a good friend at first?**

- **What happened to make the cat realize he was not behaving very nicely?**

- The horse and the dog were aware of their lack of climbing skills and so were cautious. The friendly monkey came to their rescue and offered to help them climb higher to see the splendid vision above and below them.
  Do you, like the monkey, encourage and give a helping hand to those in need?

- The cat, who was sure of his ability to jump and climb, gave advice to the horse and the dog. He told them to jump and not be afraid.
  Was this good advice by the cat?

- The cat fell and was saved by the bird. The bird could have said to the cat, "Serves you right! I'm glad you are falling!" The cat would have learnt a lesson. Instead, he saves the cat and they all become friends.
  How can you make friends with those with whom you have little in common?

- **Like our characters, is there something you want to do that will require you to be determined and work hard?**

- All wanted to climb the tree to see the world from a new perspective. They were delighted by the new world they saw beneath them and by the magnificent sky above them.
  Do you ever look in wonder at our world and see all the beauty around you?
- The tree provides a pathway to a goal. This is a difficult goal for many of our characters who are wanting to see the world in a new way.
  Have you ever climbed "trees" and seen things differently?
- The story is about friends and the values of true friendship. Notice that all the characters have their own unique talents.
  The monkey is a good climber and easily makes friends.
  The horse, although clumsy, is a philosopher and offers good advice like "You can do so much if you have a strong will". He also warns the cat not to be a 'show off'.
  The dog is gifted with a keen sense of direction and loyalty.
  The bird has the ability to fly and act swiftly.
  All our friends are talented in different ways.
  What are your talents? Do you share them with others?
- **What was your favorite part in the story?**
- **What do you think the characters next adventure will be?**

Printed in the United States
By Bookmasters